THE USBORNE BOOK OF
COUNTRIES
OF THE WORLD
FACTS

Neil Champion

CONTENTS

Designed by Stephen Meir. Joe Coonan,
Ani

Addition

Researched

D1468956

Country facts

The 5 largest countries
(square km)

Russian Federation	17,100,000
Canada	9,976,000
China	9,597,000
USA	9,363,000
Brazil	8,512,000

The 5 smallest countries
(square km)

Vatican City	0.4
Monaco	2
Nauru	21
Tuvalu	26
San Marino	61

The largest island

Greenland is the largest island. It is almost 10 times larger than Britain but only 57,000 people live there. This means that if all the people were spread out evenly, each person would have 10,000 times as much room as each person living in Britain.

Longest coastline

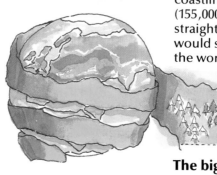

Canada has a very jagged coastline 250,000 km (155,000 miles) long. If straightened out it would stretch around the world over 6 times.

Record reigns

A six year-old boy who became Pharaoh of Egypt in 2,281 BC reigned for a record 94 years. The shortest reign was in 1908 when the King of Portugal was shot dead and his son was mortally wounded at the same time. The son survived his father as King for only 20 minutes. Japan has the longest ruling house. Present Emperor Akihito is 125th in line from Emperor Zinmu (40 to 10 BC).

The biggest desert

The world's largest desert is the Sahara. It covers part or all of 10 northern and west African countries, including Chad, Niger, Libya, Algeria, Egypt, Mali and Mauritania. It is larger than Australia, the world's sixth largest country. A person left in the desert with no water or shade would die in a day. The temperature can reach 50°C (122°F).

DID YOU KNOW?

The Vatican City, the smallest country in the world, has a population the size of a small village – 1,000 people. One hundred of these are Swiss Guards; their uniforms were designed by Michelangelo in the 15th century.

Amazing But True

Antarctica contains 70 per cent of the world's fresh water in the form of ice. In 1958, one iceberg was spotted that was thought to be the size of Belgium. Antarctica has large deposits of minerals, oil and natural gas, but it is not officially owned by any country.

The largest lake

Lake Superior in Canada is the largest lake in the world. If it were drained of all its water, the land reclaimed would cover an area twice the size of the Netherlands.

Years of education

Most countries have laws about the number of years children must spend at school. In Belgium, children attend for at least 12 years, whereas in Bangladesh and Vietnam it is 5 years.

How many countries?

There are now about 200 countries whereas in 1900 there were only 53. It is not possible to say exactly what today's figure is as there are many changes taking place world-wide.

Without a coast

There are over 30 countries without a coastline. Switzerland is one, but it still maintains its own merchant navy.

Busy frontier

More than 120 million people cross the border between Mexico and the USA every year, making it the busiest frontier. The least busy frontier used to be between East and West Germany, where the Berlin Wall once stood. The wall was pulled down in 1990.

DID YOU KNOW?

China shares its frontiers with 16 other countries:

North Korea	1.	Bhutan	11.
Russia	2.	Burma	12.
Mongolia	3.	Laos	13.
Kazakhstan	4.	Vietnam	14.
Kyrgyzstan	5.	Macau	15.
Tajikistan	6.	Hong Kong	16.
Afghanistan	7.		
Pakistan	8.		
India	9. 9a. 9b.		
Nepal	10.		

Country of islands

Indonesia is made up of over 13,000 islands, together covering about 2 million sq km (770,000 sq miles). This is equal to the area of Mexico.

Populations

Largest populations

China	1,155,800,000
India	849,640,000
USA	249,920,000
Indonesia	187,760,000
Brazil	153,320,000

Population density

Although Australia has a population 3 times larger than Hong Kong, it is 8,000 times larger in area. If the people were spread out evenly over the land each Australian would have 500,000 sq m (5,382,000 sq ft) compared with only 200 sq m (2,153 sq ft) for each person in Hong Kong.

Age distribution

In Africa almost half the population is under 15 years old and only 3 out of 100 can expect to live to 65. The situation in Europe is very different. Only one fifth of the population is under 15 and 12 in every 100 live to be 65.

DID YOU KNOW?

The population of New York, the USA's largest city, is only 3 per cent of the entire population. The population of Mexico City, Mexico's largest city, is 20 per cent of the population.

Life expectations

Men and women live to an average age of 77 years in Iceland and to an average age of 76 in both Sweden and Japan. In Yemen and Ethiopia people can expect to live about 40 years.

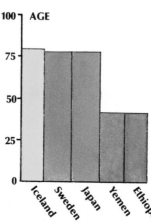

AGE chart: Iceland ~79, Sweden ~78, Japan ~77, Yemen ~40, Ethiopia ~40

Crowded countries
(people per sq km)

Macao	25,882
Monaco	15,789
Hong Kong	5,308
Singapore	4,228
Vatican City	2,500
Bermuda	1,132
Malta	1,076
Bangladesh	824
Bahrain	772
Maldives	762

More men or women?

DID YOU KNOW?

For every agricultural worker in Belgium there are at least 10 industrial workers. In Portugal there are almost as many people working on the land as there are in industry.

There are about 20 million more women than men living in Russia. This works out to a ratio of 7 women for every 6 men. But world-wide there are slightly more men than women.

Amazing But True

The world population in 1991 was over 5 billion. It is increasing daily, which means that 200 babies are born a minute. At this rate, the world's population will be over 6 billion by AD 2000.

Where no-one is born

In the Vatican City no one is born. This is because married people do not live there. It has a population that remains around 1,000. Kenya, on the other hand, has one of the highest recorded birth rates, with a 5 per cent annual increase in population. This is over twice the world-wide average.

Religions of the world

Christianity is the largest religion, with one third of the world belonging to it. Islam (Muslim) is the second largest, with 900 million worshippers (just over half the number of Christians).

The emptiest countries
(people per sq km)

Western Sahara	0.5
Mongolia	1.3
Botswana	1.9
Mauritania	1.9
Australia	2.1
Namibia	2.1
Iceland	2.4
Libya	2.4
Surinam	2.5
Canada	2.8

Amazing But True

At its present rate of increase, Honduras will double its population by the year AD 2005.

Rich and poor countries

World incomes

Half the population of the world earns a mere 5 per cent of the world's total wealth. A very rich 15 per cent takes two thirds of this wealth.

The poorest people?

By Western standards the Tasaday tribe, who live in the Philippines, are one of the poorest people in the world. They live in caves and do not keep any animals, do not grow crops, make pots or clothes or even use wheels.

How many doctors? (people per doctor)

Top 5 countries		Bottom 5 countries	
Former USSR*	235	Ethiopia	100,000
Italy	236	Burkina	42,128
Austria	256	Malawi	41,108
United Arab		Niger	40,209
Emirates	666	Burundi	20,942
UK	668		

DID YOU KNOW?

In Iceland there are 61 people on average for each hospital bed. In Bangladesh there are 4,586 people per bed, 75 times as many people for each bed as there are in Iceland.

How many people can read and write?
(per 100 people)

Top 5 countries

France	99
Italy	99
Barbados	98
USA	96
Israel	92

Bottom 5 countries

Ethiopia	9
Somalia	12
Niger	14
Afghanistan	33
Haiti	35

*Figures are not yet available for the Russian Federation.

Electricity at home

In developed countries most homes have electricity. In poorer countries many families do not. Only 3 per cent of the homes in Haiti, 18 per cent in Paraguay and Pakistan and 25 per cent in Thailand have electricity.

Pakistan

Thailand

Paraguay

Haiti

Water in our homes

In many parts of the world only a few people are lucky enough to have piped water in their homes. In countries like Afghanistan, Ethiopia and Nepal less than one in 10 homes do.

Countries in debt

Many countries have to borrow money from world banks. These countries have the biggest debts:

Brazil	$116 billion*
Mexico	$97 billion
Argentina	$61 billion
Poland	$49 billion
Nigeria	$36 billion

Amazing But True

The 400 richest citizens in the USA have a combined wealth of $288 billion*. One saw his fortune increase by $1 billion in a year. This is 12½ million times the average annual wage of a person in Bhutan.

Privately owned cars (people per car)

Top 5 countries		Bottom 5 countries	
Guam	1.1	Bangladesh	2,950
USA	1.5	Burma	1,460
Australia	2.2	Ethiopia	1,200
New Zealand	2.2	Uganda	1,425
Brunei	2.4	Somalia	950

Rich and poor countries

(To find out the average annual income for people in different countries, we have taken the wealth a country makes in a year and divided it by the number of people who live there.)

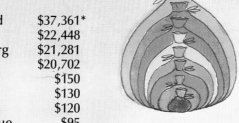

Switzerland	$37,361*
Sweden	$22,448
Luxembourg	$21,281
USA	$20,702
Bhutan	$150
Chad	$130
Ethiopia	$120
Mozambique	$95

Natural products

Top 5 wool producers
(tonnes per year)

Australia	1,100,000
Former USSR	471,000
New Zealand	304,000
China	240,000
Argentina	146,000

Most important fibre

Cotton is the world's most important fibre. It was made into cloth over 3,000 years ago in India and Central America. Today it is used to make lace, clothes, sheets, carpets, and industrial products such as thread, film, plastics and special paper.

Top 5 cotton producers
(tonnes per year)

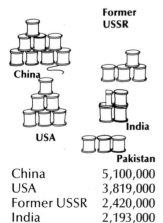

China	5,100,000
USA	3,819,000
Former USSR	2,420,000
India	2,193,000
Pakistan	1,785,000

Amazing But True

The Dutch grow and sell about 3,000 million flowers a year. This is 80,000 flowers for every sq km in the country.

Top 5 tobacco producers
(tonnes per year)

China	2,501,000
USA	732,000
India	510,000
Brazil	431,000
Former USSR	240,000

Most expensive oil

The most expensive oil used in perfumes is Musk oil. It sells at $633* for 28 g or 1 oz. It comes from glands of the male Musk deer, which are found in the mountains of Korea and Mongolia.

Fastest growing plant

Bamboo, used for making window blinds, furniture, floor mats and poles, is one of the fastest growing plants. It can shoot up 90 cms (36 ins) in a day and reaches a height of around 30 m (100 ft). It grows in India, the Far East and China.

8

*See page 48

Expensive spice

One of the most expensive spices is saffron. It comes from a crocus flower and is used to colour and give an aroma to rice dishes. Grown in China, France, Spain and Iran, over 200,000 stamens are needed to make ½ kilo (1 lb).

The secret of silk

Silk comes from the cocoon of the silkworm. One cocoon contains about a kilometre of thread. It came originally from China, where for hundreds of years its source was kept a secret. One story tells us that in 140 BC a Chinese princess hid some eggs of the silkworm in her hair and took them to Turkestan. From there silk was brought to Europe.

Top 5 rubber producers

(tonnes per year)	
Malaysia	1,300,000
Indonesia	1,200,000
Thailand	1,165,000
India	315,000
China	258,000

Amazing But True

Wild ginseng roots, found in China and Korea, sell for £10,000* for 28 g (1 oz).

DID YOU KNOW?

Tobacco was first smoked by the American Indians. It was brought to Europe in the 16th century as an ornamental plant. The habit of smoking the dried leaves did not catch on until some years later.

Where rubber comes from

Rubber comes from the sap (called latex) of the rubber tree. To drain it out, the bark has to be cut. Long before Europeans explored the jungles of Central and South America (the original home of the rubber tree) Indians were using latex to waterproof their clothes and footwear.

Best quality wool

Merino wool comes from a breed of sheep that was originally found in Spain. It is considered the best quality wool.

Fuel and energy

Top 10 coal producers
(millions of tonnes per year)

China	1,086	Australia	168
USA	823	Poland	141
Former USSR	409	UK	96
India	222	Germany	73
South Africa	177	North Korea	41

DID YOU KNOW?

More than one third of the world's population still depends on wood for fuel. In some areas of Africa and Asia, timber provides 80 per cent of energy needs. This is equivalent to the use developed nations make of gas and nuclear power.

Fuel consumption

An average American uses about 1,000 times as much fuel in his or her life as does an average Nepalese citizen and about twice as much as a European.

World's largest oil platform

The largest oil platform is the Statfjord B, built at Stavanger in Norway. It weighs 816,000 tonnes, cost £1.1 billion* to construct and needed 8 tugs to tow it into position. It is the heaviest object ever moved in one piece.

Top 10 producers of petroleum
(millions of tonnes per year)

Former USSR	584,900
USA	417,600
Saudi Arabia	327,100
Iran	155,300
Mexico	145,300
China	139,000
Venezuela	119,400
Iraq	98,200
Canada	93,300
UK	91,600

Nuclear submarines

The first nuclear-powered submarine (The Nautilus) was built in the USA in 1955. It travelled 530,000 km (330,000 miles) using only 5 kg (12 lb) of nuclear fuel. A car covering the same distance at an average speed would use 38,000 litres of petrol (8,250 gallons).

Amazing But True

If we could make use of all solar, wind, water and wave power that exists on the Earth's surface, we would have 20 billion times as much energy as we need at present.

*See page 48

Longest oil pipeline

The longest oil pipeline stretches from Edmonton, Canada, to Buffalo in New York State, USA. This is a distance of 2,856 km (1,775 miles). If it were laid out like a road, it would take a car 2 days to drive along it doing an average speed of 60 km (38 miles) an hour.

Fuels used in industry since 1850

	1850	1900	1950	2000
Wood	65%	37%	—	—
Coal	10%	55%	59%	—
Oil	—	8%	32%	15%
Gas	—	—	9%	48%
Nuclear	—	—	—	37%

Cause for alarm

By the year AD 2100 some scientists believe that the world could have run out of oil, coal and gas. This may cause some problems as it has also been estimated that we will be using 5½ times as much energy as today.

DID YOU KNOW?

Waterwheels were used in Rome over 2,000 years ago to grind corn. Water power is still used in parts of the world.

Top 10 consumers of petroleum

(millions of tonnes per year)

USA	778,900
Former USSR	402,600
Japan	245,000
Germany	126,200
Italy	92,300
France	88,700
UK	82,400
Canada	74,800
Mexico	73,845
Brazil	57,931

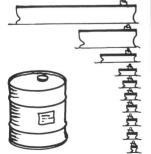

Top 5 producers of uranium (nuclear fuel)

(tonnes per year)

Canada	7,813
Australia	3,776
USA	3,000
Niger	2,964
Namibia	2,450

Amazing But True

One tonne of nuclear fuel can produce as much energy as 20,000 tonnes of coal. The first nuclear power station to produce electricity was opened in 1951 in the USA.

Metals and precious gems

World's deepest mine

The Western Deep gold mine in South Africa is 3,480 m (12,720 ft) deep. This makes it almost 9 times deeper than the tallest building is high and about 2½ times deeper than the deepest cave. It has a temperature up to 55°C (131°F) at the bottom and is cooled by special refrigerators for people working there.

Top 5 copper producers
(tonnes per year)

Chile	1,814,400
USA	1,635,400
Former USSR	900,000
Canada	777,000
Zambia	412,200

Lighter than steel

Aluminium is used to make beer and soft drink cans. A very light metal, it is replacing steel in such things as aircraft, cars, cameras, window-frames and bicycles.

Commonest precious metal

Silver is the commonest precious metal. It is lighter than gold. About half the silver mined is used as a coating for photographic film.

Largest underground mine

The San Manuel Mine in Arizona, USA, is the largest underground mine. This copper mine has over 573 km (350 miles) of tunnels. If laid out in a straight line, the tunnels would reach Los Angeles, California.

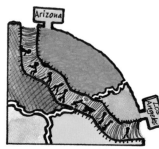

Top 5 tin producers
(tonnes per year)

China	35,800
Brazil	31,000
Indonesia	29,700
Malaysia	20,700
Former USSR	13,000

Amazing But True

South Africa produces more than twice as much gold per year as either of its nearest rivals, the former USSR and the USA. It mines 600 tonnes. 28 g of pure gold can be beaten into a fine wire, 88 km (55 miles) long.

Top 10 iron ore miners
(tonnes per year)

Former USSR	251,000,000
Brazil	131,600,000
China	100,000,000
Australia	100,000,000
India	52,000,000
USA	47,600,000
Canada	37,600,000
South Africa	22,000,000
Sweden	19,600,000
Venezuela	17,800,000

Worth its weight

Platinum is the most expensive metal in the world. Unlike silver, it does not tarnish and is used in jewellery for mounting precious gems.

Top 5 lead producers
(tonnes per year)

USA	1,291,000
Former USSR	730,000
Germany	394,000
Japan	329,000
UK	329,000

Top 5 aluminium miners
(tonnes per year)

USA	4,048,300
Former USSR	2,200,000
Canada	1,600,000
Australia	1,200,000
Brazil	930,000

USA

Former USSR

Canada

Australia

Brazil

DID YOU KNOW?

The world's most valuable gem stone is not the diamond but the ruby. The largest cut stone comes from Burma and weighs 1184 carats (one carat = 200 mgs). It is thought to be worth over $7½ million.*

*See page 48

DID YOU KNOW?

The *Cullinan*, once the largest uncut diamond, was discovered in South Africa in 1905. It was the size of a man's fist and weighed over ½ kg (1 lb). The largest gem cut from it, named the 'Star of Africa', is in the British Royal Sceptre in the Tower of London.

The oldest gems

India has records going back to 300 BC that tell us about the mining of moonstones, sapphires, diamonds, emeralds, garnets and agates.

The golden fleece

Some streams and rivers carry gold particles after running over rocks containing the precious metal. An ancient method of extracting this gold was to put a sheep's fleece in the stream, trapping the tiny pieces of metal in the wool.

A tough gem

Diamonds are 90 times harder than any other naturally occurring substance. Some are used in industry for cutting very hard substances. Dentists use them on their drills.

City of Jewels

Ratnapura, in Sri Lanka, is known as the 'City of Jewels' because of the amazing variety of gems found there. These include sapphires, diamonds and rubies.

Business and industry

Top 5 car producers
(cars per year)

Japan	9,753,000
USA	5,440,000
Germany	4,700,000
France	3,188,000
Spain	1,750,000

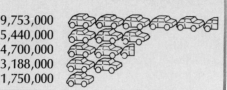

DID YOU KNOW?

China makes three times as many bicycles as its closest rivals, the USA and Japan. If the 17½ million made in a year were ridden end to end they would stretch three quarters of the way round the world.

Giant companies

Some of the world's largest companies earn more money in a year than many countries. For example, the US car giant, General Motors, has sales of around $127 billion* – more than Belgium's national income.

Stock exchanges

In stock exchanges governments and companies sell shares to raise money. There are 138 in the world at present. The oldest is in Amsterdam and dates back to 1602. The stock exchange in Tokyo holds the record for the largest amount of trading ($1,450 billion* in 1990).

The largest tanker

The *Happy Giant*, a Japanese supertanker built in 1981, is the largest tanker in the world. It is almost ½ km (a third of a mile) long, equal to about 5 football pitches end to end. It can carry 565,000 tonnes of crude oil around the world. It would take 15 of these supertankers to supply the USA with her daily needs of imported oil, or 5,500 ordinary tankers every year.

Most expensive offices

The most expensive city to rent office space in is Tokyo, where 1 sq m (11 sq ft) costs $2,600*. Even a very small company could expect to pay over $20,000 per year for floor space.

Who makes the most?
(amount produced per year)

Typewriters	Japan	2,998,000
Refrigerators	Former USSR	5,993,000
Socks	Former USSR	976,000,000
Calculators	Japan	52,435,000
Pianos	Japan	360,338

*See page 48

The power of oil

Over 30 countries in the world make money from oil export. The countries of the Middle East are thought of as big producers of oil, but Mexico, Britain, the former USSR, Nigeria and Venezuela are often forgotten. Oil accounts for one quarter of world trade.

Largest papermill

The Union Camp Corporation at Savannah, Georgia, USA, is the largest papermill, producing almost 100,000 tonnes of paper a year. This is equal to about 28,000,000 sheets of A4 paper, or 250,000 paperback books, a day.

Top 5 radio producers
(radios per year)

Hong Kong	47,986,000
China	19,990,000
Singapore	15,165,000
Japan	13,338,000
USA	11,089,000

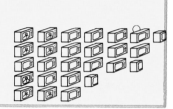

Top 5 TV producers
(sets per year)

Japan	13,275,000
USA	12,084,000
Former USSR	8,578,000
South Korea	7,641,000
China	6,840,000

The oldest company

The Faversham Oyster Fishery Company, Britain, has been going since before 1189. This makes it the oldest company on record.

Advertising products

The USA spends more money on advertising than all the other countries of the world put together. In 1978,

Amazing But True

Nippon Steel of Tokyo, Japan, produces about 27 million tonnes of steel a year. This is enough to cover all of Spain and Portugal if the steel was beaten out paper-thin.

during the Super Bowl football match final, the price of advertising on American TV was $325,000* a minute.

*See page 48

Farming

Top grain and bean producers
(tonnes per year)

Soya beans	USA	54,039,000
Barley	Former USSR	42,000,000
Corn (maize)	USA	189,867,000
Wheat	China	95,000,000
Rice	China	187,450,000

Top 5 potato growers
(tonnes per year)

Former USSR	60,000,000
China	32,553,000
Poland	32,000,000
USA	18,919,000
India	15,655,000

Top 5 banana growers
(tonnes per year)

India	6,400,000	
Brazil	5,410,000	
Philippines	3,545,000	
Ecuador	2,654,000	
Indonesia	2,400,000	

A field of wheat

About 750 years ago, an average sized field of wheat may have provided enough food for 5 people for a year. Today, the same field in a developed country would feed between 20 and 50 people for a year and supply enough seed to sow for the next crop.

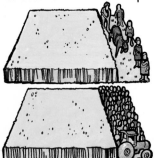

DID YOU KNOW?

The amount of protein produced from a field of soya beans is 13 times greater than the same field used to graze cattle for meat.

Largest mixed farms

Collective farming was common in the former USSR, where many people looked after their own section of a huge mixed (arable and dairy) farm. Farms could be over 25,000 hectares (62,000 acres) which is twice the size of Malta.

Top 5 beef producers
(tonnes per year)

USA	10,558,000
Former USSR	7,600,000
Brazil	2,800,000
Argentina	2,640,000
Germany	2,176,000

Top 5 cows' milk producers
(tonnes per year)

Former USSR	96,000,000
USA	67,420,000
Germany	29,800,000
India	27,000,000
France	26,600,000

A land of sheep

In Australia there are more than 3 times as many sheep as people. The largest sheep station is in South Australia. It is 1,040,000 hectares (2,560,000 acres). This is larger than Cyprus.

Top 5 grape growers
(tonnes per year)

Italy	9,300,000
France	7,020,000
Former USSR	5,400,000
Spain	5,107,000
USA	4,778,000

Top 5 sugar producers
(tonnes per year)

India	12,528,000
Former USSR	8,750,000
Brazil	8,675,000
China	7,836,000
Cuba	5,040,000

Experiments with food

What do you get when you cross the American buffalo with an ordinary cow? The beefalo of course! This animal has been bred to produce more meat to help world food production.

DID YOU KNOW?

American scientists have predicted that they will be able to breed cows weighing 4.5 tonnes. This is about the size of an elephant.

Amazing But True

A certain type of bacteria grown on petrol can be used as a source of food. The bacteria multiplies at a rate of 32,000,000 a day. It is harvested and processed into a highly nutritious food.

Top 5 butter producers
(tonnes per year)

Former USSR	1,570,000
India	1,040,000
Germany	653,000
USA	620,000
France	500,000

Forestry

Top 5 softwood log producers
(cubic metres per year)

USA	178,900,000
Former USSR	129,800,000
Canada	115,900,000
China	32,300,000
Sweden	22,400,000

Top 5 hardwood log producers
(cubic metres per year)

Brazil	34,900,000
Malaysia	31,000,000
USA	31,000,000
Indonesia	24,000,000
Former USSR	21,000,000

The tallest tree

The largest living thing on earth is the giant redwood tree, growing in the USA and Canada. The tallest is 112 m (367 ft) high. This is considerably taller than the Statue of Liberty, New York, which stands at 93 m (305 ft).

DID YOU KNOW?

The fastest growing tree in the world is the Eucalyptus. One tree in New Guinea grew 10.5 m (35 ft) in 1 year. This is almost 3 cm (over 1 in) a day. In contrast, a Sika Spruce inside the Arctic Circle takes some 98 years to grow 28 cm (11 in); some 4,000 times slower.

Forests in peril

Nearly half the world's rain forests have been cut down and are still being cut down at a rate of 24 sq km (9 sq miles) an hour or 200,000 sq km (80,000 sq miles) a year – an area almost the size of Britain.

The rubber tree

Rubber trees were originally found only in the Amazon rain forest. In 1876 Sir Henry Wickham shipped 70,000 seeds to Kew Gardens in London. Seedlings were then sent to Sri Lanka and Malaysia where rubber plantations were started.

World's largest forest

About 25 per cent of the world's forests cover an area of the Russian Federation and Scandinavia and extend as far as the Arctic Circle. It is the world's largest forest.

World of trees

There are about 40 million sq km (15 million sq miles) of forest in the world. This is more than the total area of the Russian Federation, Canada and China.

The oldest tree

Some bristlecone pines found in California, USA, are over 4,500 years old.

Top 5 producers of paper and board
(tonnes per year)

USA	71,519,000	🗐🗐🗐🗐🗐🗐🗐🗐🗐🗐
Japan	28,086,000	🗐🗐🗐🗐
Canada	16,466,000	🗐🗐🗐
China	13,719,000	🗐🗐
Germany	11,873,000	🗐🗐

A tree of gold

In 1959 a nursery in the USA bought a single Golden Delicious apple tree for $51,000 (at the time, £18,214),* making it the most expensive tree the world has known.

The lightest wood

Wood from the Balsa tree weighs 40 kg per cubic metre (2½ lb per cubic ft). It is the world's lightest wood. The black ironwood tree is forty times heavier.

Amazing But True

In Borneo (Indonesia), a fire raged non-stop for 10 months from September 1982. It covered over 36,000 sq km (14,000 sq miles) and about 13,500 sq km (5,000 sq miles) of forest was destroyed. Several rare species of trees and wildlife were made extinct.

*See page 48

Fishing

Freezer trawlers

Fish caught at sea are often frozen on board the trawlers. They are gutted and left in piles to freeze together. Once back in port, they are defrosted, filleted and sold.

Top fish-eating nation

The Japanese eat their way through 3,400 million kg (7,500 million lbs) of fish a year. This means that each person has an average 30 kg (65 lbs) of fish a year. They are the world's biggest fish-eating nation. Their nearest rivals, the Scandinavians, eat only half as much fish on average and the Americans only one fifth.

Amazing But True

Over 95 per cent of all the fish caught in the world are caught in the northern hemisphere.

DID YOU KNOW?

A special substance found in the scales of some fish (especially herrings) is used to make a paint. This paint is coated on to glass beads to make imitation pearls.

The most expensive fish

The Russian sturgeon fetches the highest price of any fish in the world. The eggs of the female sturgeon (caviare) are a prized delicacy. The best caviare costs over £28* for 50 g (1¾ ozs) or £570 per kg (£258 per lb).

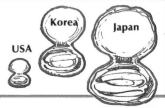

Top 5 most caught fish
(millions of tonnes per year)

Alaska Pollack	4.5
Japanese Pilchard	4
Chilean Pilchard	3.25
Atlantic Cod	2.25
Chilean Jack Mackerel	2

Top 3 oyster catchers
(tonnes per year)

Japan	250,288
Korea	189,204
USA	81,336

*See page 48

Greatest catch

The most fish ever caught in one haul was made by a Norwegian trawler. It is estimated that in one net it pulled on board more than 120 million fish; over 2,400 tonnes in all. This is enough to feed every man, woman and child in Norway for two weeks.

Fish farming

Many countries now breed fish in special underwater farms. These are the leading countries in this sort of farming:

(in tonnes per year)

China	2,300,000
India	600,000
Former USSR	300,000
Japan	250,000
Indonesia	240,000

Largest fishing vessel

A whaling factory ship built in the former USSR in 1971, called *The Vostok*, weighs 26,400 tonnes, making it the largest fishing vessel in the world. It is 224.5 m (736.5 ft) long, which means that you could fit 9½ tennis courts end to end along its deck.

Fishing with birds

In Japan, cormorants are trained to catch fish and to fly back to a boat. Each bird is stopped from swallowing the fish by a tight leather collar around its neck.

DID YOU KNOW?

Out of all the fish caught in the world, about three quarters are eaten as food. The other quarter is used to make such things as glue, soap, margarine, pet food and fertilizer.

Amazing But True

A prehistoric fish that was thought to have become extinct about 70 million years ago, was caught in the sea off South Africa. It is called the coelacanth and since 1938 many more of these fish have been caught.

Top 5 fishing countries
(tonnes per year)

Japan	11,841,000	
Former USSR	11,159,000	
China	9,346,200	
USA	5,736,000	
Chile	4,814,400	

Food and drink

How many calories?

Calories measure the energy content of different foods. We all need a certain amount every day to make our bodies work properly. People in Europe and the USA eat about 3,500 calories a day. Many people in Africa and Asia have at most 1,600. Some people in these countries live on a very poor diet. This may consist of beans, vegetables and grains, and may be too low in calories and protein.

Top 5 wine producers
(tonnes per year)

France	6,200,000
Italy	6,000,000
Spain	3,107,000
Argentina	2,100,000
USA	1,580,000

Top 5 beer producers
(tonnes per year)

USA	23,655,000
Germany	11,806,000
China	6,926,000
Japan	6,232,000
UK	6,006,000

A world-wide drink

There are about 200 countries in the world and Coca-cola is sold in 185 of them. Every day 492 million servings are consumed. If all the cans sold in one month were placed on top of each other they would make three chains, each reaching the moon.

DID YOU KNOW?

The largest cake ever weighed over 58 tonnes. It was baked in the USA in 1989 to celebrate the 100th birthday of Fort Payne, Alabama.

Meals within meals

Bedouin sometimes prepare a meal of stuffed, roast camel for wedding feasts. They start by stuffing a fish with eggs, putting this inside a chicken, the chicken inside a whole roast sheep and the lot inside a cooked camel.

Most nutritious fruit

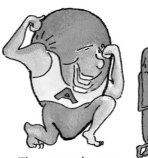

The avocado pear contains about 165 calories for every 100 g of edible fruit. This is more than eggs or milk. It also contains twice as much protein as milk, and more vitamin A, B and C. In contrast, the cucumber has only 16 calories per 100 gms.

Most expensive food

L'Aquila white truffles from France cost £22.40* for 28 g (1 oz), which is equivalent to £780 per kg (£358 per lb).

Top 5 honey producers
(tonnes per year)

Former USSR	240,000	
China	190,000	
USA	91,000	
Mexico	52,700	
Argentina	44,000	

Top 5 tea producers
(tonnes per year)

India	742,000	
China	546,000	
Sri Lanka	247,700	
Kenya	203,600	
Turkey	135,000	

Top 5 coffee producers
(tonnes per year)

Brazil	1,286,000	
Colombia	870,000	
Indonesia	408,000	
Mexico	299,000	
Ivory Coast	240,000	

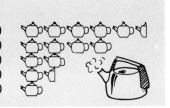

A monster melon

The largest melon weighed over 90 kg (14 stone). The size of a large human being, it would have fed 400 people.

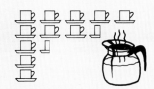

Super sausage

A sausage-maker in Birmingham, Britain, made one specimen that was 9 km (5½ miles) long. This amounts to about 87,000 ordinary sausages.

*See page 48

Buildings and structures

The largest hotel

The world's largest hotel is the Excalibur Hotel and Casino in Nevada, USA. It has 4,032 deluxe rooms, 7 restaurants, and employs 4,000 staff. It opened in April 1990 and cost $290 million*.

DID YOU KNOW?

The most expensive hotel in the world is the Fairmont Hotel in San Francisco, USA. It costs $6,000* plus tax per night. This includes a butler and a maid, and a limousine service.

World's longest wall

The Great Wall of China stretches for 3,460 km (2,150 miles), ranges between 4½ and 12 m (15 and 40 ft) high, and is up to 10 m (32 ft) thick. Another 2,860 km (1,780 miles) can be added because of spurs and kinks. This makes it as long as the River Nile, the longest river in the world. Six Great Walls laid end to end would reach round the circumference of the Earth.

The largest palace

The Imperial Palace in the middle of Peking, China, covers an area of 72 hectares (178 acres). This is equal to 100 football pitches. It is surrounded by the largest moat in the world – 38 km (23½ miles) in length.

The tallest buildings

Sears Tower, Chicago, USA	443 metres
World Trade Centre, New York, USA	411 metres
Empire State Building, New York, USA	381 metres
Standard Oil Building, Chicago, USA	346 metres
John Hancock Center, Chicago, USA	343 metres
Chrysler Building, New York, USA	319 metres
60 Wall Tower, New York, USA	290 metres
First Canadian Place, Toronto, Canada	289 metres
40 Wall Tower, New York, USA	282 metres
Bank of Manhattan, New York, USA	274 metres

Highest homes

The highest settlement is on the Indian and Tibetan border. Basisi is 5,988 m (19,650 ft) above sea level. This is only 2,860 m (9,384 ft) lower than Mount Everest, the highest mountain in the world.

*See page 48

The highest dam

The highest dam is in Russia. Completed in 1990, the Rogunsky dam towers 335 m (1098 ft) high. This is higher than the Grande Dixence in Switzerland which is only 15 m (50 ft) short of the Eiffel Tower.

The tallest lighthouse

The steel tower lighthouse in Yokohama, Japan, is 106 m (348 ft) high. But almost 7 of these would be needed standing on top of each other to reach the world's tallest structure, the Warszawa Radio Mast in Poland.

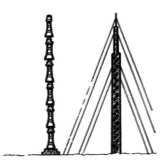

The oldest buildings

Twenty-one huts were discovered in 1960 in Nice, France, that have been dated to 400,000 BC. They are the oldest recognizable buildings in the world.

Smallest house

A fisherman's cottage in North Wales has only 2 tiny rooms and a staircase inside. The outside measures 1.8 m (6 ft) wide and only just over 3 m (10 ft) high.

Seven Wonders

The Seven Wonders of the World were first mentioned in the 2nd century BC by a man called Antipater of Sidon. They were:

The Pyramids of Giza, Egypt
The Hanging Gardens of Babylon, Iraq
The Tomb of King Mausolus, Turkey
The Temple of Diana, Ephesus, Turkey
The Colossus of Rhodes, Greece
The Statue of Jupiter, Olympia, Greece
The Pharos of Alexandria, Egypt

Of the Seven Wonders, only the pyramids are still standing. The others have been destroyed by fire, earthquake and invading nations.

DID YOU KNOW?

The longest bridge span in the world is the Humber Estuary Bridge, Britain. It is 1,410 m (4,626 ft) across. It was opened in 1981, having taken 9 years to build.

Cities

Fastest growing city

Mexico City is growing at a rate of 25 per cent every 5 years. With a population of over 19 million, it is estimated, that by the year 2000 it will be over 31 million. This is 5 times as many people as there are in Switzerland at present.

The largest town

Mount Isa, Queensland, Australia, spreads over almost 41,000 sq km (15,800 sq miles). It covers an area 26 times greater than that of London and is about the same size as Switzerland.

Top 10 most crowded cities
(people per city)

Mexico City	19,400,000
New York	18,000,000
Los Angeles	13,500,000
Cairo	13,000,000
Shanghai	12,500,000
Peking	10,700,000
Seoul	9,700,000
Calcutta	9,200,000
Moscow	8,800,000
Paris	8,700,000

Traffic City

The greatest amount of vehicles in any city is to be found in Los Angeles, USA. At one interchange almost 500,000 vehicles were counted in a 24-hour period during a weekday. This is an average of 20,000 cars and trucks an hour.

The cheapest city

In 1626 a Dutchman bought an island in America from some local Indians. He gave them some cloth and beads worth about $24* for an area of land he thought covered 86 sq km (34 sq miles). In fact it was 57 sq km (22 sq miles). But it was still a bargain. He had bought Manhattan, now one of the most crowded and expensive islands in the world. He named his town New Amsterdam but it was later renamed New York.

How many people live in cities?

About one third of people in the world live in towns or cities. By the year 2000, experts believe that over half will live in urban areas. But this may vary from place to place. In the USA about 74 per cent live in towns and cities compared with 20 per cent in India.

*See page 48

The oldest city

Archaeologists believe that Jericho, in Jordan, is the oldest continuously inhabited place. There were as many as 3,000 people living there as early as 7,800 BC.

Longest underground

London has 400 km (247 miles) of underground tracks, making it the longest in the world. This includes 267 stations and about 450 trains. All the track laid end to end would stretch from London to Land's End in Cornwall.

An island city

Venice, in the north of Italy, is built on 118 islands in a lagoon. Canals serve as streets and roads and everybody uses boats instead of cars to get around. There are over 400 bridges crossing the canals.

Poles apart

The most northerly capital is Reykjavík in Iceland. The southern-most is Wellington, New Zealand. They are 20,000 km (12,500 miles) apart.

The longest name

Krung Thep is the shortened name of the capital of Thailand, known in the West as Bangkok. Its full name has 167 letters and means in English,

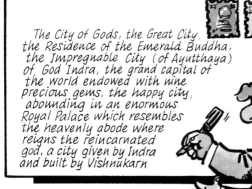

The City of Gods, the Great City, the Residence of the Emerald Buddha, the Impregnable City (of Ayutthaya) of God Indra, the grand capital of the world endowed with nine precious gems, the happy city, abounding in an enormous Royal Palace which resembles the heavenly abode where reigns the reincarnated god, a city given by Indra and built by Vishnukarn

So far from the sea

Urungi, capital of the Uighur Autonomous Region in China, is the furthest city from the sea. It is about 2,250 km (1,400 miles) from the nearest coast.

Communications

Telephones – top 5 countries
(per 1,000 people)

Monaco	1250
Liechtenstein	1000
Bermuda	909
Sweden	909
Switzerland	883

Televisions – top 5 countries
(per 1,000 people)

USA	785
Bermuda	709
Guam	672
Monaco	630
Japan	562

Longest telephone cable

A telephone cable running beneath the Pacific Ocean links Canada and Australia via New Zealand and the Hawaiian Islands. It is 14,500 km (9,000 miles) long and cost £35 million* in 1963 to build.

Largest and smallest book

The smallest published book measures 1 x 1 mm (0.004 x 0.004 in) and is called *Old King Cole*. Only 85 copies were printed by Gleniffer Press of Scotland. Over 4 million copies would fit on the cover of the world's largest book (the *Super Book*) which measures 2.74 x 3.07 m (9 x 10 ft).

Secret codes

Coded messages have been used since 400 BC. Probably the best known is the Morse code, invented in the 19th century by Samuel Morse.

Newspapers – top 9 countries

(bought daily per 1,000 people)

Japan	575
Liechtenstein	558
Germany	530
Sweden	524
Finland	515
Norway	483
Britain	421
Iceland	420
Monaco	410

Dates of famous inventions

Telephone	1876
Gramophone	1877
Moving film	1885
Television	1934
Audio film	1927
Tape recorder	1935
Photocopier	1938
Computer	1946
Transistor radio	1948
Stereo recording	1958
Microcomputer	1969

Crossed wires

The Pentagon, Washington DC, is the centre of American defence. It has the largest switchboard in the world. About 25,000 telephone lines can be used at the same time.

*See page 48

Mail bag

The USA has the largest postal service in the world. In one year its citizens sent over 120 billion letters and packages. This is equal to 521 letters a year or about 1½ letters a day, for everyone living in America.

Communicating flags

Semaphore is a method of signalling with flags. With one flag in each hand, the signaller holds them in different positions to spell out the alphabet. A way of passing messages over a short distance, it was invented by the French army in 1792 during the French Revolution.

Computers for speech

The *Sprite* is a piece of computer technology that has been designed to imitate the human voice. It helps those with speech problems.

A long-distance chat

Men have talked to each other directly between the moon and the earth, a distance of 400,000 km (250,000 miles), making this the longest distance chat. A powerful radio signal sent into space is expected to take 24,000 years to reach its destination, a group of stars 10 billion times further away than the moon. It could be the longest awaited reply.

A golden pen

The ballpoint pen was invented in 1938 by a Hungarian named Biro. In its first year in the UK 53 million were sold.

Newspaper facts

When *The Times* newspaper reported Nelson's victory over the French at the Battle of Trafalgar in 1805, the news took 2½ weeks to reach London. When the same newspaper, 164 years later, showed pictures of the first men on the moon, they came out only a few hours after the landing.

DID YOU KNOW?

The world's first postage stamp was the *Penny Black*, issued in Britain in May, 1840. A one-cent British Guiana (Guyana) stamp of 1856, of which there is only one example, is thought to be worth £500,000*.

Shrinking world

Using satellites orbiting the earth, television can now reach a potential audience of about 2½ billion people. An event like the Olympic Games, can be beamed live into the homes of half the people in the world.

*See page 48

Travel

Airship travel

Hydrogen-filled airships were in regular use up until 1938, taking people across the Atlantic. They were stopped because too many caught fire.

Road building

To move their armies the Romans built over 80,000 km (50,000 miles) of road in Europe and the Middle East. After their conquest of Britain, it took only 6 days by horse to get from London to Rome. About 1,500 years later in the 19th century, it took just as long.

Most travelled person

An American, named Jesse Rosdall, went to all the countries and territories in the world except North Korea and the French Antarctic. He claimed to have travelled a total of 2,617,766 km (1,626,605 miles). This is equal to almost 7 trips to the moon or 65 journeys round the world.

Petrol consumption

In the USA, over 1,364 million litres (300 million gallons) of petrol are used each day – enough petrol in a year to fill an oil drum 36.5 km (22.7 miles) high and 26.5 km (16.5 miles) wide. This would fill Lake Baikal in Russia, the lake with the greatest volume.

Top 5 road countries
(km of road)

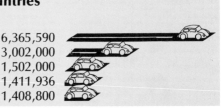

USA	6,365,590
Canada	3,002,000
France	1,502,000
Brazil	1,411,936
Former USSR	1,408,800

Longest and shortest flight

The shortest scheduled flight (from the island of Westray to Papa Westray off Scotland, lasting 2 minutes) could be made over 450 times while one jet makes a non-stop journey from Sydney to San Francisco, a total of 7,475 km (4,645 miles).

The first car

The first petrol-driven car took to the roads in 1885. It had 3 wheels and a tiller to steer. Its top speed was 16 km/h (10 mph). Just 100 years later there are enough vehicles in the world for every tenth person to own one. If they all met in one traffic jam, it would go round the world 34 times.

DID YOU KNOW?

Concorde travels faster than the speed of sound, cruising at 2,333 km/h (1,500 mph). It flies between London and New York in 3 hours, a distance of 5,536 km (3,500 miles). This is over twice as fast as an ordinary passenger plane.

Widest and narrowest

The widest road in the world is the Monumental Axis in Brasília, Brazil. It is 250 m (820 ft) wide, which is wide enough for 160 cars side by side. It is over 500 times wider than the narrowest street, which is in Port Issac, Britain. At its narrowest it is a mere 49 cm (1½ ft) and is known as 'squeeze-belly alley'.

World famous train

The Orient Express once ran between Paris and Istanbul. It now makes a shorter trip from London to Venice. It offers luxury travel at £1,500* for a return ticket. This is twice the price of a return plane ticket to Sydney, Australia, a city 14 times further away from London than Venice.

Busiest rail network

About 18½ million people use trains in Japan every day. If one train carried them all, it would have about 370,000 carriages and would stretch for over 3,300 km (2,000 miles).

Fastest train

The French railway system operates the TGV train, which achieved a top speed of 515 km/h (320 mph) without passengers in 1990. Its average speed on the Paris to Lyon passenger route is 212.5 km/h (132 mph).

Top 5 railway countries
(km of track)

USA	296,497
Former USSR	144,900
Canada	120,000
Germany	83,244
India	61,478

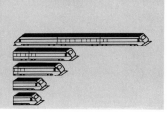

Amazing But True

The Boeing 747 (Jumbo Jet) is the largest and most powerful plane. It can carry up to 500 passengers. It stands as high as a 6-storey office block and weighs over 370 tonnes. It has a maximum speed of 969 km/h (602 mph) and a wing-span of over 70 m (232 ft).

The bicycle

An early form of bicycle, called a hobbyhorse or walk-along, was popular in the mid-17th century. It had no pedals. We had to wait almost 200 years for their invention.

Top holiday countries
(number of visitors)

France	51,462,000
USA	39,772,000
Spain	34,300,000
Italy	26,679,000
Hungary	20,510,000
Austria	19,011,000
UK	18,021,000
Germany	17,045,000
Canada	15,258,000
Switzerland	13,200,000

*See page 48

Money*

World's largest mint

The largest mint – the factory where coins are made – is in the USA. It can make 22 million coins a day using almost 100 stamping machines. It covers an area of 4½ hectares (11 acres). At full production it could produce a pile of coins 5 times higher than Mount Everest in just one day.

Earliest coins

Coins found in Lydia (Turkey) date from the reign of King Gyges in the 7th century BC. These coins below were found in Sicily and date to the 5th century BC.

Highest value note

A few, very rare, $10,000* notes exist in America. They are not in general circulation.

In 1989, Britain's Abbey National Building Society handed over a cheque worth £1,425,000,000* to the newly created Abbey National plc. It was the largest cheque ever written.

Military spending

The USA spends $300 billion* on defence in a year – more than the people in most countries earn collectively in the same period. The USA and the former USSR used to spend more on arms than all the rest of the world.

Highest paid job

Michael Milken, an American working for Drexel Burnham Lambert Inc., earned $15,000* a day in salary and bonuses in 1987 – an annual income of $550 million.

Sunken treasure

Almost 2,000 Spanish galleons lie off the coast of Florida and the Bahamas. They were sunk in the 16th century, most of them carrying large amounts of gold. This area is the largest untapped storehouse of treasure in the world.

Golden Beatle

Paul McCartney, songwriter and ex-Beatle, earns an estimated £25 million a year from his records. This is about £45* a minute or £70,000* a day.

*See page 48

The Chinese one kwan note printed in the 14th century was 92.8 x 33 cm (9 x 13 in). It is 73 times larger than the smallest note, the 10 bani issued in Romania in 1917.

Income Tax

Many governments take a certain amount of money from the salaries of their citizens. This is called Income Tax. It was introduced in Britain in 1799 by the Prime Minister, William Pitt. He needed money to pay for the war against Napoleon. The war ended over 150 years ago, but Income Tax has remained.

Different money

Coins and notes are not the only form of money. Teeth of animals, metal bracelets and necklaces, shells, axe heads, knives, blocks of salt and even blocks of tea leaves have been used. The word *cash* comes from an Indian word meaning compressed tea and the word *salary* comes from the Latin word for salt. Both were used to pay people in the past.

Honesty rules

In 1972, $500,000* was found by Lowell Elliot in Indiana, USA. The money was dropped by a criminal escaping by parachute. Resisting the temptation to keep the money, he tracked down the owner and returned every cent.

Powerful banks

The world's most wealthy bank is Citicorp, based in New York. Only the US Government handles more money in a year. The 56 poorest countries each has less wealth than each of the top 500 commercial banks in the world.

Money loses value

When the price of buying things goes up, money becomes worth less. This is called inflation. In Germany after the First World War, the German Mark dropped in value. In 1921, 81 Marks were worth 1 American dollar. Two years later, the same dollar was worth 1 million Marks.

Great Train Robbery

In 1963 over £2½ million* was stolen from a train in Buckinghamshire, England. Only one seventh of the total was ever recovered. It was the costliest train robbery.

*See page 48

Languages

10 most spoken languages

Chinese	700,000,000
English	400,000,000
Russian	265,000,000
Spanish	240,000,000
Hindustani	230,000,000
Arabic	146,000,000
Portuguese	145,000,000
Bengali	144,000,000
German	119,000,000
Japanese	116,000,000

The first alphabet

The Phoenicians, who once lived where Syria, Jordan and Lebanon are today, had an alphabet of 29 letters as early as 1,700 BC. It was adopted by the Greeks and the Romans. Through the Romans, who went on to conquer most of Europe, it became the alphabet of Western countries.

Sounds strange

One tribe of Mexican Indians hold entire conversations just by whistling. The different pitches provide meaning.

The Rosetta Stone

The Rosetta Stone was found by Napoleon in the sands of Egypt. It dates to about 196 BC. On it is an inscription in hieroglyphics and a translation in Greek. Because scholars knew ancient Greek, they could work out what the Egyptian hieroglyphics meant. From this they learned the language of the ancient Egyptians.

Many Chinese cannot understand each other. They have different ways of speaking (called dialects) in different parts of the country. But today in schools all over China, the children are being taught one dialect (Mandarin), so that one day all Chinese will understand each other.

Translating computers

Computers can be used to help people of different nationalities, who do not know each others' language, talk to each other. By giving a computer a message in one language it will translate it into another specified language.

World-wide language

English is spoken either as a first or second language in at least 45 countries. This is more than any other language. It is the language of international business and scientific conferences and is used by airtraffic controllers world-wide. In all, about one third of the world speaks it.

Earliest writing

Chinese writing has been found on pottery, and even on a tortoise shell, going back 6,000 years. Pictures made the basis for their writing, each picture showing an object or idea. Probably the earliest form of writing came from the Middle East, where Iraq and Iran are now. This region was then ruled by the Sumerians.

The most words

English has more words in it than any other language. There are about 1 million in all, a third of which are technical terms. Most people only use about 1 per cent of the words available, that is, about 10,000. William Shakespeare is reputed to have made most use of the English vocabulary.

Amazing But True

A scientific word describing a process in the human cell is 207,000 letters long. This makes this single word equal in length to a short novel or about 80 typed sheets of A4 paper.

Many tongues

A Frenchman, named Georges Henri Schmidt, is fluent (meaning he reads and writes well) in 31 different languages.

International language

Esperanto was invented in the 1880s by a Pole, Dr Zamenhof. It was hoped that it would become the international language of Europe. It took words from many European countries and has a very easy grammar that can be learned in an hour or two.

The same language

The languages of India and Europe may originally come from just one source. Many words in different languages sound similar. For example, the word for *King* in Latin is *Rex,* in Indian, *Raj,* in Italian *Re,* in French *Roi* and in Spanish *Rey.* The original language has been named Indo-European. Basque, spoken in the French and Spanish Pyrenees, is an exception. It seems to have a different source which is still unknown.

Number of alphabets

There are 65 alphabets in use in the world today. Here are some of them:

Roman
ABCDEFGHIJKLMNOPQRS

Greek
ΑΒΓΔΕΖΗΘΙΚΛΜΝΞΟΠΡ

Russian (Cyrillic)
АБЬВГДЕЖЗИЙІКЛМНОП

Hebrew
מעדיף כיום דיור בשירות

Chinese
評定,因此我們制定一種申請房屋計劃游

Arabic
١٨٩٧ وصل إلى إنجلترا أنموذج

Art and entertainment

Most productive painter

Picasso, the Spanish artist who died in 1973, is estimated to have produced over 13,000 paintings, as well as a great many engravings, book illustrations and sculptures, during his long career – he lived to be 91. This means that he painted an average 3½ pictures every week of his adult life.

Most valuable painting

Leonardo da Vinci's *Mona Lisa* is probably the world's most valuable painting. It was stolen from the Louvre, Paris, in 1911, where it had hung since it was painted in 1507. It took 2 years to recover. During that time, 6 forgeries turned up in the USA, each selling for a very high price.

The oldest museum

The Ashmolean Museum in Oxford, Britain, was built in 1679.

The record of records

The *Guinness Book of Records*, first published in 1955, has been translated into 24 languages and has sold over 50 million copies world-wide.

Largest painting by a single artist

The Battle of Gettysburg by Paul Philippoteaux is the size of 10 tennis courts. It took 2½ years to paint (1883) and measures 125 m (410 ft) by 21.3 m (70 ft).

Largest art gallery

The Winter Palace and the Hermitage in St Petersburg, Russia, have 322 galleries showing a total of 3 million works of art and archaeological exhibits. A walk around all the galleries is 24 km (15 miles).

Best-selling novelist

Barbara Cartland, a British authoress, has sold about 500 million copies of her romantic novels world-wide and they have been translated into 17 languages. All her books gathered together would make 5,000 piles, each as high as the Eiffel Tower.

Pop records

The Beatles were the most successful pop group of all time. They sold over 1,000 million discs and tapes. The biggest selling single was *White Christmas*, written by Irving Berlin and sung by Bing Crosby. The most successful album is *Thriller* by Michael Jackson, selling over 40 million copies.

Band Aid

On July 13th, 1985, two pop concerts took place, one in Wembley, London, and the other at the JF Kennedy Stadium, Philadelphia. Fifty well-known bands played to raise money for the starving of Africa. By the end of the year over £50 million* had been raised by the concert, together with a record and a book of the event.

Largest audiences

The largest audience for a single concert was in 1990 when an estimated 2 million people attended a Bastille Day concert by Jean-Michel Jarre. The Rolling Stones attracted record audiences to their 1989 *Steel Wheels* tour of North America. 3.3 million people attended in 30 cities, raising a record £185 million*.

DID YOU KNOW?

The smallest professional theatre in the world is to be found in Hamburg, Germany. *The Piccolo* seats only 30 people. The Perth Entertainment Centre, Australia, has a theatre that holds 80,000, which is a capacity over 2,500 times greater.

William Shakespeare

Shakespeare, commonly thought the world's greatest playwright, wrote 37 plays in all. The longest is *Hamlet*. The role of Hamlet is also the longest written by Shakespeare.

A night at the opera

Richard Wagner had an eccentric patron in Ludwig II, King of Bavaria. He was so impressed by Wagner's music that he built a castle (called Neuschwanstein) in Bavaria for Wagner's operas.

Most expensive film

The most expensive film ever made was *Terminator 2: Judgement Day*. It cost $104 million* to make.

Amazing But True

Wolfgang Amadeus Mozart wrote about 1,000 pieces of music, including many operas and symphonies. He died aged 35, but had been composing since the age of 4. He is thought to be one of the world's greatest composers.

*See page 48

The world of machines

Largest and slowest

The machine that takes the Space Shuttle to its launching pad is called the *Crawler* and for a very good reason. It weighs 3,000 tonnes and travels at a maximum speed of 3 km/h (2 mph). It is 40 m (130 ft) long, and 35 m (115 ft) wide.

Oldest working clock

The mechanical clock in Salisbury Cathedral, Britain, dates back to 1386. It is still in full working order, after repairs were made in 1956, some 600 years later.

Earliest steam engine

Richard Trevithick, a Cornish inventor, built the first steam engine in 1803. The first public railway was opened 23 years later between Stockton and Darlington, Britain. The engine used was designed by George Stephenson.

The sewing machine

The sewing machine was first used in France in the early 19th century. It was made of wood. Isaac Singer invented the first foot treadle machine in 1851. This became so popular that it lead to mass-production of sewing machines.

Amazing But True

The Scottish inventor, John Logie Baird, gave the first public demonstration of the television in 1926 in Soho, London. Ten years later there were 100 TV sets in the country. Today there are about 100 million sets in the USA alone.

DID YOU KNOW?

The first motorcycle was designed and built by the firm of Michaux-Perreaux in France in 1869. It ran on steam and had a top speed of 16 km/h (10 mph). The first petrol-driven motorcycle was designed in 1885 by Gottlieb Daimler. Its top speed was 19 km/h (12 mph). Compare this with the 512 km/h (318.6 mph) of the fastest modern bike.

Radio fraud

In 1913, almost 50 years after the first radio transmission, an American was convicted of trying to mislead the public. He had advertised that in a few years his radio company would be able to transmit the human voice across the Atlantic to Europe. The district attorney did not believe him. Two years later a trans-Atlantic conversation took place.

A mirror on the universe

The inventor of the telescope is thought to be Roger Bacon, a 13th century monk. His instrument was first discovered in detail in 1608 by a Dutchman. Today, the largest telescope is the Keck telescope on Mauna Kea, in Hawaii. It has a 10 m (33ft) mirror made up of 36 segments, all joined together to make the correct curve.

Powerful computer

The fastest and most powerful computer is the liquid-cooled Cray 2, which has a main memory capacity of 32 million bytes. If all the people in China could each make a calculation in a second, it would take the entire population to keep up with this computer.

Most powerful fire-engine

A fire-engine designed to tackle aircraft fires can squirt 277 gallons of foam a second out of its 2 turrets. It is the 8-wheeled Oshkosh firetruck. It could fill an olympic-sized swimming pool in only 30 minutes.

Most accurate clock

The Olsen clock in Copenhagen town hall, Denmark, will lose half a second every 300 years. It took 10 years to make. An atomic clock in the USA is accurate to within 1 second in 1,700,000 years.

The fastest official record for typing is 216 words in one minute or 3½ words per second. An electronic printer in the USA can type over 3,000 times faster: that is 700,000 words a minute or 12,000 a second.

The longest cars

In 1927, 6 Bugatti 'Royales' were made in France. They were each 6.7 m (22 ft) long. A custom built Lamrooster measures 15.24 m (50 ft), has 10 wheels and a pool in the back.

World speed records

Steam locomotive	1938	202.77 km/h	(126.00 mph)
Helicopter	1986	400.87 km/h	(249.09 mph)
Motorcycle	1978	512.73 km/h	(318.60 mph)
Aircraft	1976	3,529.00 km/h	(2,192.9 mph)
Command module	1969	39,897.00 km/h	(24,791.5 mph)

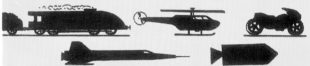

World map

Alaska

Canada

Greenland

Finland

Sweden

Iceland   Norway

Britain

Ireland

6

1

2   **3**

8   **5**

France   **9**   **10**
16 15

17   Italy

Portugal

Spain

United States of America

ATLANTIC OCEAN

Morocco

Tunisi

Bermuda

Algeria   Libya

Bahamas

Mexico

Dominican Republic

Western Sahara

Cape Verde

Cuba

Puerto Rico

Belize

Haiti   Dominica

Mauritania

Mali

Niger

Guatemala

Honduras

Nicaragua

Gambia   Senegal

32

33

El Salvador

Barbados

Guinea-Bissau

Nigeria

Costa Rica

Trinidad and Tobago

Guinea

Panama

Venezuela

Guyana

Sierra Leone

34

Surinam

Liberia

Benin

Colombia

French Guiana

Ivory Coast   Togo   **30**

PACIFIC OCEAN

Ghana

Gabon

Ecuador

Congo

KEY TO NUMBERS

Peru

Brazil

Angola

1 Denmark
2 Germany
3 Poland
4 Slovak Republic
5 Czech Republic
6 Netherlands
7 Belgium
8 Luxembourg
9 Switzerland
10 Austria
11 Hungary
12 Romania
13 Yugoslavia
14 Bosnia-Herzegovina
15 Croatia
16 Slovenia
17 Andorra
18 Bulgaria
19 Albania
20 Greece

Bolivia

Paraguay

Chile

Uruguay

Argentina

Falkland Islands

Namibia

Botswana

South Africa

21 Syria
22 Lebanon
23 Israel
24 Jordan
25 Kuwait
26 Bahrain
27 Qatar
28 United Arab Emirates
29 Bangladesh
30 Cambodia
31 Singapore
32 Burkina
33 Chad
34 Cameroon
35 Central African Republic
36 Equatorial Guinea
37 Uganda

ARCTIC OCEAN

Russian Federation

Kazakhstan

Mongolia

7
8

49
Turkey 50 51 52 53 55
54

2 21
23 24 Iraq Iran
Afghanistan
China
N. Korea
Japan
S. Korea

25 26 Pakistan
27 28 Nepal Bhutan
gypt Saudi Oman Laos Taiwan
Arabia India Burma Hong Kong
Sudan 29 Vietnam Philippines
Yemen 30
Djibouti Thailand Brunei
Ethiopia Maldives Sri Lanka
aire Somalia Malaysia Papua New Guinea
37 Kenya 31 Solomon
38 Seychelles Indonesia Islands
39 Tanzania
Comoros INDIAN OCEAN
41 Mauritius Fiji
40 Reunion
42 Madagascar Australia
Mozambique
Swaziland
Lesotho New Zealand

38 Rwanda
39 Burundi
40 Malawi   48 Moldavia
41 Zambia   49 Georgia
42 Zimbabwe   50 Armenia
43 Estonia   51 Azerbaijan
44 Latvia   52 Turkmenistan
45 Lithuania   53 Uzbekistan
46 Belorussia   54 Tajikistan
47 Ukraine   55 Kyrgyzstan

Countries of the world facts

Country	Capital	Population	Area (sq km)	Area (sq miles)
Afghanistan	Kabul	16,430,000	648,000	250,000
Albania	Tiranë	3,300,000	29,000	11,000
Algeria	Algiers	25,660,000	2,382,000	919,500
American Samoa	Pago Pago	47,000	197	76
Andorra	Andorra	60,000	500	193
Angola and Cabinda	Luanda	10,020,000	1,247,000	481,500
Anguilla	The Valley	8,000	96	37
Antigua and Barbuda	St John's	77,000	442	171
Argentina	Buenos Aires	32,710,000	2,767,000	1,068,000
Armenia	Yerevan	3,300,000	30,000	11,500
Aruba	Oranjestad	62,500	193	75
Australia	Canberra	17,340,000	7,678,000	2,964,000
Austria	Vienna	7,820,000	84,000	32,500
Azerbaijan	Baku	7,000,000	87,000	33,500
Bahamas	Nassau	253,000	14,000	5,500
Bahrain	Manama	520,000	600	232
Bangladesh	Dacca	118,740,000	144,000	55,500
Barbados	Bridgetown	255,000	430	166
Belgium	Brussels	9,840,000	31,000	12,000
Belize	Belmopan	188,000	23,000	9,000
Belorussia	Minsk	10,000,000	207,500	80,000
Benin	Porto Novo	4,736,000	113,000	43,500
Bermuda	Hamilton	61,000	50	19
Bhutan	Thimphu	1,550,000	47,000	18,000
Bolivia	La Paz	7,610,000	1,099,000	424,000
Bosnia-Herzegovina	Sarajevo	4,364,500	51,500	20,000
Botswana	Gaborone	1,350,000	600,000	231,500
Brazil	Brasília	153,320,000	8,512,000	3,285,500
Brunei	Bandar Seri Begawan	270,000	6,000	2,500
Bulgaria	Sofia	8,980,000	111,000	43,000
Burkina	Ouagadougou	9,240,000	274,000	106,000
Burma	Rangoon	42,560,000	676,500	261,000
Burundi	Bujumbura	5,458,000	28,000	11,000
Cambodia	Phnom Penh	8,440,000	181,000	70,000
Cameroon	Yaoundé	11,834,000	475,000	183,500
Canada	Ottawa	26,603,000	9,976,000	3,851,000
Cape Verde	Praia	370,000	4,000	1,500
Cayman Islands	Georgetown	27,000	300	116
Central African Republic	Bangui	3,039,000	623,000	240,500
Chad	Ndjamena	5,687,000	1,284,000	495,500
Chile	Santiago	13,390,000	757,000	292,000
China	Peking	1,155,800,000	9,597,000	3,704,500
Colombia	Bogotá	33,610,000	1,139,000	439,500
Comoros	Moroni	551,000	2,000	772
Congo	Brazzaville	2,271,000	342,000	132,000
Costa Rica	San José	2,994,000	51,000	19,500
Croatia	Zagreb	4,760,500	56,500	22,000
Cuba	Havana	10,625,000	115,000	44,500
Cyprus	Nicosia	710,000	9,000	3,500
Czech Republic	Prague	10,400,000	79,000	30,500
Denmark	Copenhagen	5,150,000	43,000	16,500

Country	Capital	Population	Area (sq km)	Area (sq miles)
Djibouti	Djibouti	409,000	22,000	8,500
Dominica	Roseau	83,000	751	290
Dominican Republic	Santo Domingo	7,170,000	49,000	19,000
Ecuador	Quito	10,850,000	284,000	109,500
Egypt	Cairo	53,223,000	1,001,000	386,500
El Salvador	San Salvador	5,252,000	21,000	8,000
Equatorial Guinea	Malabo	348,000	28,000	11,000
Estonia	Tallinn	1,600,000	45,000	17,500
Ethiopia	Addis Ababa	53,380,000	1,222,000	471,500
Falkland Islands	Stanley	2,000	12,000	4,500
Fiji	Suva	780,000	18,000	7,000
Finland	Helsinki	5,030,000	337,000	130,000
France	Paris	57,050,000	551,000	212,500
French Guiana	Cayenne	100,000	91,000	35,000
Gabon	Libreville	1,172,000	268,000	103,500
Gambia	Banjul	861,000	11,000	4,000
Georgia	Tbilisi	5,460,000	69,700	27,000
Germany	Berlin	79,360,000	357,000	138,000
Ghana	Accra	15,028,000	239,000	92,000
Greece	Athens	10,060,000	132,000	51,000
Greenland	Godthåb	57,000	2,186,000	844,000
Grenada	St George's	80,000	344	133
Guadeloupe	Basse-Terre	344,000	2,000	772
Guam	Agana	132,000	541	209
Guatemala	Guatemala City	9,197,000	109,000	42,000
Guinea	Conakry	5,756,000	246,000	95,000
Guinea-Bissau	Bissau	965,000	36,000	14,000
Guyana	Georgetown	800,000	215,000	83,000
Haiti	Port-au-Prince	6,486,000	28,000	11,000
Honduras	Tegucigalpa	5,105,000	112,000	43,000
Hong Kong	Hong Kong	5,750,000	1,000	386
Hungary	Budapest	10,340,000	93,000	36,000
Iceland	Reykjavík	260,000	103,000	40,000
India	Delhi	849,640,000	3,288,000	1,269,000
Indonesia	Jakarta	187,760,000	1,904,000	735,000
Iran	Tehran	57,730,000	1,648,000	636,000
Iraq	Baghdad	19,580,000	435,000	168,000
Ireland	Dublin	3,520,000	70,000	27,000
Israel	Jerusalem	4,970,000	21,000	8,000
Italy	Rome	57,050,000	301,000	116,000
Ivory Coast	Abidjan	11,998,000	322,000	124,500
Jamaica	Kingston	2,420,000	11,000	4,000
Japan	Tokyo	123,920,000	372,000	143,500
Jordan	Amman	4,140,000	98,000	38,000
Kazakhstan	Alma-Ata	16,691,000	2,717,500	1,049,000
Kenya	Nairobi	24,032,000	583,000	225,000
Kiribati	Tarawa	70,000	717	277
Korea, North	Pyongyang	22,190,000	121,000	47,000
Korea, South	Seoul	43,270,000	98,000	38,000
Kuwait	Kuwait City	2,100,000	18,000	7,000
Kyrgyzstan	Bishkek	4,400,000	76,500	29,500

Country	Capital	Population	Area (sq km)	Area (sq miles)
Laos	Vientiane	4,260,000	237,000	91,500
Latvia	Riga	2,680,000	25,000	9,500
Lebanon	Beirut	2,740,000	10,000	4,000
Lesotho	Maseru	1,774,000	30,000	11,500
Liberia	Monrovia	2,607,000	111,000	43,000
Libya	Tripoli	4,545,000	1,760,000	679,500
Liechtenstein	Vaduz	30,000	160	62
Lithuania	Vilnius	3,700,000	65,000	25,000
Luxembourg	Luxembourg	370,000	3,000	1,000
Madagascar	Antananarivo	11,197,000	587,000	226,500
Malawi	Lilongwe	8,289,000	118,000	45,500
Malaysia	Kuala Lumpur	18,330,000	330,000	127,500
Maldives	Malé	220,000	300	116
Mali	Bamoko	8,156,000	1,240,000	478,500
Malta	Valletta	360,000	300	116
Martinique	Fort-de-France	340,000	1,000	386
Mauritania	Nouakchott	2,025,000	1,031,000	398,000
Mauritius	Port Louis	1,075,000	2,000	772
Mexico	Mexico City	86,154,000	1,973,000	761,500
Moldavia	Chişhinău	4,400,000	33,700	13,000
Monaco	Monaco	30,000	2	0·8
Mongolia	Ulan Bator	2,250,000	1,567,000	605,000
Morocco	Rabat	25,061,000	447,000	172,500
Mozambique	Maputo	15,656,000	783,000	302,000
Namibia	Windhoek	1,781,000	824,000	318,000
Nauru	Nauru	9,350	21	8
Nepal	Kathmandu	19,600,000	141,000	54,500
Netherlands	Amsterdam	15,060,000	37,000	14,500
Netherlands Antilles	Willemstad	190,000	800	309
New Caledonia	Noumea	170,000	22,000	8,500
New Zealand	Wellington	3,380,000	269,000	104,000
Nicaragua	Managua	3,871,000	130,000	50,000
Niger	Niamey	7,732,000	1,267,000	489,000
Nigeria	Lagos	108,542,000	925,000	357,000
Norway	Oslo	4,260,000	324,000	125,000
Oman	Muscat	1,560,000	212,000	82,000
Pakistan	Islamabad	115,520,000	804,000	310,500
Panama	Panama City	2,418,000	77,000	30,000
Papua New Guinea	Port Moresby	3,770,000	462,000	178,500
Paraguay	Asunción	4,400,000	407,000	157,000
Peru	Lima	22,000,000	1,285,000	496,000
Philippines	Manila	62,870,000	300,000	116,000
Poland	Warsaw	38,240,000	313,000	121,000
Portugal	Lisbon	10,580,000	92,000	35,500
Puerto Rico	San Juan	3,599,000	9,000	3,500
Qatar	Doha	380,000	11,000	4,000
Réunion	Saint-Denis	592,000	3,000	1,000
Romania	Bucharest	23,190,000	238,000	92,000
Russian Federation	Moscow	148,500,000	17,075,500	6,591,000
Rwanda	Kigali	7,181,000	26,000	10,000
St Kitts and Nevis	Basseterre	44,600	265	102
St Lucia	Castries	150,000	600	232
St Vincent-Grenadines	Kingstown	120,000	389	150
San Marino	San Marino	20,000	61	24

Country	Capital	Population	Area (sq km)	Area (sq miles)
São Tomé and Principe	São Tomé	121,000	1,000	386
Saudi Arabia	Riyadh	14,870,000	2,150,000	830,000
Senegal	Dakar	7,327,000	196,000	75,500
Seychelles	Victoria	70,000	440	170
Sierra Leone	Freetown	4,151,000	72,000	28,000
Singapore	Singapore	2,710,000	600	232
Slovak Republic	Bratislava	5,300,000	49,000	19,000
Slovenia	Ljubljana	1,950,000	20,500	8,000
Solomon Islands	Honiara	320,000	29,000	11,000
Somalia	Mogadishu	7,497,000	638,000	246,500
South Africa	Pretoria	35,282,000	1,221,000	471,500
Spain	Madrid	38,960,000	505,000	195,000
Sri Lanka	Colombo	16,990,000	66,000	25,500
Sudan	Khartoum	25,204,000	2,506,000	967,500
Surinam	Paramaribo	420,000	163,000	63,000
Swaziland	Mbabane	770,000	17,000	6,500
Sweden	Stockholm	8,560,000	450,000	174,000
Switzerland	Berne	6,710,000	41,000	16,000
Syria	Damascus	12,120,000	185,000	71,500
Taiwan	Taipei	19,910,000	36,000	14,000
Tajikistan	Dushanbe	5,000,000	143,000	55,000
Tanzania	Dar-es-Salaam	25,635,000	945,000	365,000
Thailand	Bangkok	56,080,000	514,000	198,500
Togo	Lomé	3,531,000	56,000	21,500
Tonga	Nuku'alofa	90,000	800	309
Trinidad and Tobago	Port of Spain	1,230,000	5,000	2,000
Tunisia	Tunis	8,074,000	164,000	63,500
Turkey	Ankara	56,100,000	781,000	301,500
Turkmenistan	Ashkhabad	3,600,000	488,000	188,500
Tuvalu	Funafuti	10,000	26	10
Uganda	Kampala	18,795,000	236,000	91,000
Ukraine	Kiev	51,700,000	604,000	233,000
United Arab Emirates	Abu Dhabi	1,590,000	87,000	33,500
United Kingdom	London	57,410,000	244,000	94,000
USA	Washington DC	249,920,000	9,363,000	3,614,000
Uruguay	Montevideo	3,100,000	176,000	68,000
Uzbekistan	Tashkent	20,000,000	447,500	172,500
Vanuatu	Vila	150,000	15,000	6,000
Vatican City	Vatican City	1,000	0.4	0·1
Venezuela	Caracas	19,320,000	912,000	352,000
Vietnam	Hanoi	66,230,000	330,000	127,500
Virgin Islands	Road Town	17,000	130	50
Western Sahara	Ad Dakhla	179,000	267,000	103,000
Western Samoa	Apia	200,000	3,000	1,000
Yemen	Sana'a	11,280,000	528,000	204,000
Yugoslavia	Belgrade	10,337,500	102,000	39,500
Zaire	Kinshasa	35,562,000	2,345,000	905,000
Zambia	Lusaka	8,073,000	753,000	290,500
Zimbabwe	Harare	9,369,000	391,000	151,000

Index

---

* **Currency conversion chart (correct on October 8th, 1992)**

	US$	Sing.$	NZ$	Aust.$	Can.$	£ Sterling
US$	1.0	1.59	1.85	1.39	1.24	0.57
Singapore $1	0.63	1.0	1.16	0.88	0.77	0.36
New Zealand $1	0.54	0.86	1.0	0.75	0.67	0.31
Australian $1	0.72	1.14	1.33	1.0	0.89	0.42
Canadian $1	0.81	1.29	1.50	1.12	1.0	0.47
£1 Sterling	1.73	2.75	3.18	2.38	2.13	1.0